W9-CTS-428

PEANUTS®

LINUS
Gets Glasses

by Charles M. Schulz

adapted by Sheri Tan

illustrated by Robert Pope

Ready-to-Read

Simon Spotlight

New York London Toronto Sydney New Delhi

SIMON SPOTLIGHT
An imprint of Simon & Schuster Children's Publishing Division
1230 Avenue of the Americas, New York, New York 10020
This Simon Spotlight edition December 2016
© 2016 Peanuts Worldwide LLC
All rights reserved, including the right of reproduction in whole or in part in any form.
SIMON SPOTLIGHT, READY-TO-READ, and colophon are registered trademarks of Simon & Schuster, Inc.
For information about special discounts for bulk purchases, please contact Simon & Schuster Special Sales at
1-866-506-1949 or business@simonandschuster.com.
Manufactured in the United States of America 1116 LAK
2 4 6 8 10 9 7 5 3 1
ISBN 978-1-4814-7725-3 (hc)
ISBN 978-1-4814-7724-6 (pbk)
ISBN 978-1-4814-7726-0 (eBook)

Charlie Brown and Linus
are walking home from school
when all of a sudden
Linus stops and points ahead.
"Look out, Charlie Brown!"
he shouts. "There's a queen snake!"

Charlie Brown checks.
"That's not a snake.
It's just an old stick,"
he says.

Linus warns Charlie Brown
not to pick it up anyway.
"Some queen snakes can
appear very sticklike," Linus says.

They continue walking
until Linus walks into a tree.

"Ouch!" Linus says.
"Where did that mailbox
come from?"

The tree, which is most
definitely not a mailbox,
has been there a long time.
For Charlie Brown the clues add up.
"Linus, I think you are having
some eye trouble.
Maybe you should speak
to a professional," he says.

Linus decides to
follow Charlie Brown's advice.
But the professional he speaks to
isn't as professional as he seems.
It's Snoopy!

"No offense, Linus, but maybe you should talk to a real doctor," Charlie Brown says.

Snoopy looks at his diploma.
According to Ace Obedience School,
I'm a Doctor of Napping.
Doesn't that count for anything?
Snoopy thinks.

Linus finally goes to
the eye doctor's office.
"All right, I'm ready.
Give me the most difficult
eyesight test you've got!"
Linus says.

But everything on the
exam looks blurry.
"How about your second
most difficult eyesight test?"
Linus suggests.

It's official.
Linus needs glasses.

Linus tries on his new glasses.
"Not bad at all," he thinks.

On the walk home
Linus is amazed.
He can see everything clearly.
The sticks look like sticks,
and the trees look like trees.
"I've never noticed how lovely
this tree is before!" Linus says.
"It must be new."

At home Linus looks
inside the fridge.

Even the apple looks tastier.
Linus takes it out.
Chomp!

"I don't know how this is possible, but not only can I see things better, I can taste things better, too!" Linus says.

Everything is going well.
Then Lucy gets home.

Lucy looks in the fridge and
sees the apple isn't there.
"Linus, did you eat my apple?"
she hollers.
Linus smells trouble.

Thankfully, Linus is a quick thinker.
"Now that I have glasses, I can see
things a lot more clearly.
Like for instance, how smart and
pretty my big sister, Lucy, is,"
he says.

Lucy frowns.
Even though Linus got glasses,
he is still as sarcastic as ever!

But then Lucy does something else.
She stops being mad.
She looks into Linus's glasses
and says,
"Those look very nice on you, Linus."

Lucy smiles and fluffs her hair.
She can see her reflection
in the lenses!

Later Linus visits Charlie Brown.
"I am so happy you talked me into
seeing the eye doctor, Charlie
Brown," he says.
"I love wearing my glasses.
Not only can I see better,
but they also make me look
smart and spiffy."

Snoopy likes to look
smart and spiffy too.

It looks like Linus might need
a second pair of glasses!